DUDLEY SCHOOLS
LIBRARY SERVICE

KU-086-636

Schools Library and Information Services

S00000796259

DUDLEY	
SCHOOLS LIBRARY SERVICE	
S00000796259	
£12.99	J966
29-Mar-2017	PETERS

Explore!
BENIN

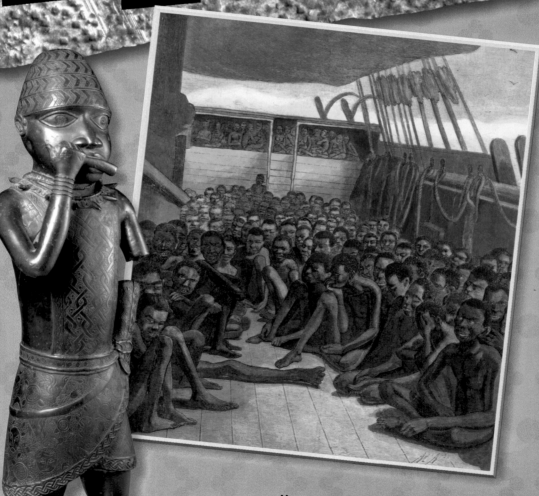

Izzi Howell

WAYLAND
www.waylandbooks.co.uk

First published in Great Britain in 2017 by Wayland

Copyright © Hodder and Stoughton Limited, 2017

All rights reserved.

ISBN 978 1 5263 0084 3
10 9 8 7 6 5 4 3 2 1

MIX
Paper from responsible sources
FSC® C104740

Wayland
An imprint of Hachette Children's Group
Part of Hodder & Stoughton
Carmelite House
50 Victoria Embankment
London EC4Y 0DZ

An Hachette UK Company
www.hachette.co.uk
www.hachettechildrens.co.uk

A catalogue record for this title is available from the British Library

Printed and bound in China

Produced for Wayland by
White-Thomson Publishing Ltd
www.wtpub.co.uk

Editor: Izzi Howell
Designer: Clare Nicholas
Illustrations: Julian Baker
Wayland editor: Hayley Shortt
Consultant: Philip Parker

Every effort has been made to clear image copyright. Should there be any inadvertent omission, please apply to the publisher for rectification.

Picture acknowledgements:
The author and publisher would like to thank the following agencies and people for allowing these pictures to be reproduced:

Alamy /Granger Historical Picture Archive 8; Brooklyn Museum title page (left), 17 (left); Brooklyn Museum 5 (top); Brooklyn Museum 10; Brooklyn Museum 11 (right); Brooklyn Museum 20; Brooklyn Museum 21 (top right); i-Stock/kira_an 14; i-Stock/Gitanna 18; LACMA/gift of Ann Bing Arnold (M.74.90) 22; Shutterstock title page (right); Shutterstock/Eduard Kyslynskyy 4 (top left); Shutterstock/tristan tan 4 (top right); Shutterstock/Svetlana Foote 4 (bottom left); Shutterstock/imfoto 4 (bottom right); Shutterstock/pyzata 6; Shutterstock/Luriya Chinwan 9 (bottom); Shutterstock/Rich Carey 12; Shutterstock/bonhan 13 (top); Shutterstock/anat chant 13 (centre); Shutterstock/gilkop 13 (bottom); Shutterstock/Everett Historical (bottom); Shutterstock/Anton_Ivanov 19 (centre); Shutterstock/Utopia_88 (bottom); Shutterstock/Panom 21 (bottom); Shutterstock/Alena Brozova 23; Shutterstock/tanewpix 26; Shutterstock/Tatiana Volgutova 28; Shutterstock/Armita 28; Superstock/DeAgostini 27 (top); Werner Forman Archive/Museum fur Volkerkunde, Berlin cover (top left); Werner Forman Archive/British Museum, London cover (top right) and 5 (bottom); Werner Forman Archive/Courtesy Entwistle Gallery, London cover (centre right); Werner Forman Archive/late Herbert Rieser Collection cover (bottom); Werner Forman Archive/British Museum, London 7; Werner Forman Archive/Museum fur Volkerkunde, Berlin 9 (top); Werner Forman Archive/British Museum, London 11 (left); Werner Forman Archive/British Museum, London 16; Werner Forman 17 (right); Werner Forman Archive/National Commission for Museums and Monuments, Lagos 19 (top); Werner Forman 21 (top left); Werner Forman Archive/British Museum, London 24; Werner Forman Archive 27 (bottom); Wikimedia/Collectie Stichting National Museum van Wereldculturen 15.

All design elements from Shutterstock.

Please note:
The website addresses (URLs) included in this book were valid at the time of going to press. However, because of the nature of the Internet, it is possible that some addresses may have changed, or sites may have changed or closed down since publication. While the author and publishers regret any inconvenience this may cause to the readers, no responsibility for any such changes can be accepted by either the author or the publishers.

Contents

What was Benin?

Some of the goods that Benin sold to European traders included leopard skins, palm oil, ivory and precious stones, such as sapphires.

B enin was one of the most important kingdoms in West Africa in the 15th and 16th centuries. It became wealthy through trade with Europe and conquered neighbouring land.

Trade

Trade was very important in the Benin Kingdom, as the money earned from trade was used to pay for their large, powerful army. They were able to buy guns from European traders, which put them at an advantage over other people in the area. Benin's soldiers also kidnapped people from conquered lands, whom they sold into the slave trade.

The Benin bronzes

Benin is famous for its bronze plaques, which hung in the king's palace in Benin City, the capital city of Benin. These plaques were made by skilled craftsmen. Craftsmen decorated the plaques with images of life in Benin, such as soldiers, traders and the king of Benin (the Oba).

This bronze plaque made in Benin shows a Portuguese trader wearing European-style armour.

How do we know?

As the people of Benin passed on their history through spoken stories, rather than written records, we don't have much written evidence about the Benin Kingdom. However, we can learn a lot about wars, festivals and palace life from bronze plaques and other artefacts. We can also read reports written by European traders who visited Benin.

This bronze plaque from the 17th century shows the Oba riding on horseback. This shows us that important people used horses for transport in the Benin Kingdom.

The rise of Benin

In roughly 500 years, Benin grew from a scattered community of people to a powerful kingdom. The founders and inhabitants of Benin were the Edo, an ethnic group of people from West Africa.

The first kingdom

In around 900 CE, the Edo people started to live together in small family groups. Over time, these groups became a kingdom named Igodomigodo. It is believed that Igodomigodo was ruled by kings called Ogisos, but as there are no written records about this period, it's hard to know the exact details.

The Edo people lived in the rainforests of the area that is known today as Nigeria.

Ogisos and Obas

In the 12th century, the Ogisos lost control of Benin. The Edo invited a prince from the nearby Yoruba kingdom to rule over them. The prince's son, Eweka, became the first Oba of Benin. Oba means 'king' in Yoruba. Eweka's son became Oba after his death, and he was followed by many more Obas.

This is a brass model of the head of an Oba. His coral necklace and woven cap are signs of his wealth and power.

SAHARA

AFRICA

IFE/OYO KINGDOM
C. 1200–1835
(YORUBA PEOPLE)

BENIN KINGDOM
C. 900–1897
(EDO PEOPLE)

ATLANTIC OCEAN

A mighty kingdom

Under the rule of the Oba Ewuare the Great (ruled c.1440 to 1480), Benin grew into a powerful kingdom. This was the beginning of the golden age of Benin. Benin became rich through trade with Portuguese merchants. They used this money to pay for a large army, which seized land and helped the kingdom to expand.

This map shows the size and location of the Benin Kingdom and the nearby Ife/Oyo Kingdom.

Benin City

There are almost no remains of Benin City, the capital city of the Benin Kingdom. Most of what we know comes from accounts written by European visitors from the 15th century onwards.

A magnificent city

European visitors were very impressed by Benin City. Most European cities at that time were cramped and dirty, while Benin City was grand, spacious and clean. Reports from the time described streetlights fuelled by palm oil and drains in the road to carry away excess rainwater. One visitor wrote that crime was so rare that most houses didn't even have doors.

This drawing of Benin City is from 1668. Historians aren't sure how accurate this drawing is, as the artist had only heard reports of what the city looked like.

python

Portuguese traders

Palaces and houses

All buildings in Benin City were made from clay. The Oba lived in a vast palace at the centre of the city. Inside the palace, there were large courtyards and pillars decorated with hundreds of intricate bronze plaques. Ordinary people lived in large houses with many rooms. They decorated their walls by polishing the clay and cutting horizontal lines into them.

This plaque shows the entrance to the Oba's palace. The entrance is decorated with a python and the faces of Portuguese traders, and is protected by four guards.

High walls

Benin City was surrounded by tall earth walls, which helped the inhabitants to defend their city. The walls also continued beyond the city limits, dividing the surrounding area into small villages. In places, these walls were 20 metres high.

None of the walls of Benin City remain today. This is a modern earth wall, made by pressing layers of earth tightly together. The walls in Benin City probably looked similar to this.

Society

It's hard to know what life was like for ordinary people living in the Benin Kingdom. Most of the evidence that we have, such as written records and plaques, focuses on the lives of powerful, wealthy people such as the Oba.

Chiefs and officials

The Oba ruled with the help of different chiefs and officials. The Uzama, or elders, were the king's most important advisors. Palace chiefs from rich families ran the royal court and organised deals with merchants. Town chiefs, who ruled over villages, were chosen for their leadership skills. When the Benin army conquered land, local chiefs could continue to rule over their area, as long as they sent tribute to the Oba.

This pendant shows the Oba (centre) with two important court officials.

Town and country

Most people in the countryside worked as farmers. Skilled craftsmen could find lots of work in Benin City, making objects from wood, metal, leather and ivory. Craftsmen who worked with the same materials formed guilds and lived together in the same area.

This is part of a large intricately-carved ivory bell made by craftsmen that was used in a religious ceremony.

Women

Most women in Benin probably spent their time cooking, cleaning and taking care of their families. However, historians think that some women worked as craftswomen, making pottery in Benin City. The most important woman in Benin was the Iyoba, or mother of the Oba. The Iyoba had political power and her own large palace.

This ivory pendant is a portrait of Queen Idia, the first Iyoba. She was given the title after helping her son win a war and become the Oba.

11

Food and farming

Farmers in the Benin Kingdom grew crops on cleared rainforest land and hunted for wild meat and fish. They ate some of the food themselves and sold the best-quality produce to wealthy people who did not farm.

Farmers in the Benin Kingdom had to clear areas of the rainforest to make space to plant their crops.

Farming the land

All the land in the Benin Kingdom belonged to the Oba. Farmers were allowed to grow crops and live on the land, but they could not own it. There was not much natural farmland so farmers grew crops in cleared areas of the rainforest.

yams

okra

The Benin diet
The most important crop in the Benin Kingdom was the yam, a root vegetable similar to a sweet potato. Ordinary people probably ate yams at every meal. People cooked using palm oil, made from the fruit of oil palm trees. Later, European traders introduced new ingredients that they had brought back from South America, such as chilli peppers, tomatoes and peanuts.

As well as yams, farmers in Benin grew okra, beans, melons and peppers.

Meat and hunting
Ordinary people in Benin ate meat when it was available. Some people kept chickens, cows and goats. Men hunted wild animals, such as deer, antelopes and rabbits, with traps, bows and arrows and spears. The Oba allowed a few people to hunt elephants and leopards for their ivory and skins.

Only men hunted for animals, such as gazelles, but both men and women took part in fishing.

Trade

The first Portuguese traders arrived in Benin in 1485, looking for gold to buy. Although Benin had no gold to sell, they supplied Portugal with other exotic items and slaves.

Goods for sale

Benin sold natural resources and crafts to Portuguese traders. We think that they sold large quantities of finely carved ivory objects, many of which were decorated with images of Portuguese traders. Although some of these goods were produced in Benin, many were bought from people who lived in nearby kingdoms and then sold on to the Europeans for a profit.

One of the most popular traded goods was a type of pepper that could not be grown in Europe.

Metal and guns

Benin bought metal from European traders, which they used to create the plaques that decorated the Oba's palace. Luxury items, such as coral and fabrics, were also popular imports. Although Benin was keen to buy guns from Portuguese traders, Portugal refused for many years, as Benin was not a Christian country. Benin was finally allowed to buy guns in the 17th century.

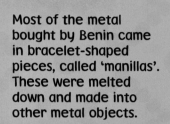

Most of the metal bought by Benin came in bracelet-shaped pieces, called 'manillas'. These were melted down and made into other metal objects.

The slave trade

Benin's army captured people from neighbouring kingdoms to sell as slaves. These slaves were taken to work in other parts of Africa and in Brazil, which was ruled by Portugal at that time. At first, Benin only sold female slaves, but by the late 17th century, they had started to sell men as well. The slave trade was so profitable that Benin even sold its own citizens as slaves.

Slave traders transported slaves on large ships. On board, the slaves lived in very bad conditions and were not given clothes to wear or space to move around.

15

Armies and weapons

B enin had a large, powerful army, which seized land from nearby kingdoms and captured slaves for trade.

Weapons

At first, most soldiers fought with weapons such as brass and iron swords, spears and wooden crossbows, which were typical weapons across West Africa. In the 15th century, Portuguese traders brought guns to Benin. Although they did not sell guns to the Benin Kingdom at first, some Portuguese men with guns joined Benin's army as paid soldiers.

This plaque shows a Portuguese soldier armed with a gun. Neighbouring armies, who relied on traditional weapons, would have had no chance against these soldiers.

Armour and shields

Ordinary soldiers carried shields made from wood, woven fibres and animal skins and wore thick protective clothing. Powerful army leaders wore wooden helmets that were covered with tough crocodile skin. They protected their bodies with leopard skins, which were thick enough to stop arrows.

▶ The large figure in the centre of this plaque is probably an important chief. He is dressed for battle with a helmet, bow and sword and is surrounded by servants.

Scaring the enemy

Benin's army played musical instruments as they went into battle to scare their opponents. Each soldier carried a bell, which they played together to make a confusing ringing noise. Some soldiers played loud horns.

Horns were also played at court to entertain the Oba and his officials.

Religion and beliefs

Religion was an important part of life in Benin. The people of Benin had many beliefs and myths about humans, gods and animals.

Only the Oba and a few of his chiefs could wear precious coral jewellery, bought from European traders. The Edo believed that an ancient Oba won the right to wear coral after beating the god Olokun in a wrestling match.

Gods and rulers

The Edo believed that the Ogisos and the Obas were descended from the god Osanobua, who created the world. Ogisos and Obas were also worshipped as gods and were believed to have great magical powers. Gods such as Ogun, the god of iron and war, and Olokun, the god of water, ruled over other areas of life.

Celebrating festivals

Religious festivals in Benin followed the working year, celebrating different seasonal events such as harvest, as well as the Oba and the gods. Everyone in the kingdom had a part to play in the festival, from making costumes and objects for rituals to growing food for feasts.

This plaque shows two men performing a ritual dance at a festival to honour the god of war, Ogun. The dancers are using ropes as part of their dance.

Animals and humans

The people of Benin divided humans and animals into an order based on their power. At the top of the order was the Oba, the most important and powerful person on Earth, followed by all other humans and then animals. Animals, such as cows, were often sacrificed.

Some animals had symbolic meanings. The crocodile was used to represent the Oba, as both had the power to kill people. The python was a symbol of Olokun, the god of water.

19

Art

B enin is best known for its intricate bronze plaques and sculptures, but craftsmen also produced beautiful carvings made from ivory and wood.

Plaques and statues

Benin's bronze plaques show scenes of Obas and chiefs, historical events and wars. They originally hung on pillars in the Oba's palace. Craftsmen also made large bronze heads, which were placed on altars that honoured previous Obas. Obas placed offerings on these altars in religious ceremonies to honour their ancestors.

The bronze heads were not portraits of the deceased Oba. They just show the typical features of someone from Benin, dressed in the fine jewellery of an Oba.

Ivory

Carved ivory objects were made for the Oba and to sell to European traders. Some of the ivory objects made for trade were decorated with images of European traders, noblemen and ships. Ivory objects that were kept in Benin were usually decorated with traditional images.

◄ This ivory salt cellar has Portuguese noblemen at the bottom and a caravel, a Portuguese ship, at the top.

► This carved tusk was probably used in religious rituals. Carved tusks were often placed on top of the bronze heads in altars.

European impressions

Although Portuguese traders bought crafts from Benin, their art was not well known in Europe until the end of the 19th century. After British troops destroyed Benin City in 1897 (see page 27), they brought back thousands of bronze plaques and objects. Many people in Europe at the time were shocked by the intricate details and beauty of the artworks from Benin, as they didn't believe that African societies could create sophisticated pieces of art. Later, African art was an important inspiration for many modern artists.

This is a waxwork of the Spanish artist Pablo Picasso with one of his paintings. Picasso was very inspired by African art and masks in the early 20th century.

A day in the life

The Oba employed many craftsmen, who produced luxury items for his palace. Many of these craftsmen lived in a section of the Oba's palace, alongside people who made similar objects. This fictional diary entry describes what it might have been like to work as a craftsman in the Oba's palace.

I wake up with the sunrise and eat a quick breakfast of yams and fresh fruit. Today, my guild is going to work on some new plaques for the Oba, showing his recent victory against a neighbouring tribe. I am very honoured that I have been chosen to make a plaque showing the Oba.

First, I need to make the wax model. I take a large block of wax from the storeroom and start carving out the design with a blade. In the centre is an image of the Oba, dressed in a leopard skin and coral beads and holding a large sword. I add a crocodile at his feet as a sign of his power.

Bronze plaques were often decorated with delicate patterns as well as figures of humans and animals.

Now, I can make a clay mould of the model. I leave the mould to dry in the hot sun while I take a break. I walk around the metalworkers' section of the palace and eat a bowl of rabbit stew.

When the mould is dry, I remove the wax. I fetch some metal manillas from the storeroom and heat them until they melt. With the help of another worker, I pour the molten liquid into the mould until it is full. Then I leave the metal to harden overnight. Tomorrow morning, I will open the mould and check that the plaque is good enough to be presented to the Oba.

Metal must be heated to a very high temperature before it melts into a liquid and can be poured into a mould.

The diary entry on these pages has been written for this book. Can you create your own diary entry for another person who lived in the Benin Kingdom? It could be an Oba or a farmer. Use the facts in this book and in other sources to help you write about a day in their life.

Make your own leopard statue

The leopard was an important animal in the culture of Benin. They were used as a symbol of the Oba's royal power because the leopard is thought to be the 'king' of their habitat. In the 17th century, the Oba even kept tame leopards that walked in ceremonial processions. You can make your own leopard statue from air-drying clay.

These ivory leopard statues are from the 19th century. They were placed on either side of the Oba's throne on important occasions.

You will need:

a large ball of air-drying clay

a modelling tool

a paintbrush

yellow paint

black paint

1 Separate your clay into one large ball, one medium ball and five small balls. Roll the large ball and the small balls into logs.

2 Use your modelling tool to attach the medium ball to the top of one end of the large log. Attach four small logs as legs and one small log as the tail.

3 Use your modelling tool to shape the face of the leopard. Add ears and eyes. Leave your statue to dry according to the instructions on the clay packet.

4 Once the leopard is dry, paint it with yellow paint. Use the black paint for dots and details, such as whiskers.

Handy hint
You could mix your yellow paint with white paint to match the colour of the original leopard statues.

The British invasion

Much of the Benin Kingdom was destroyed by British troops at the end of the 19th century. Many valuable artefacts were stolen from the Benin territory, which is part of Nigeria today.

Controlling resources

In the 19th century, European countries such as France, Britain and Belgium started to take control of large areas of Africa. They wanted access to valuable natural resources, which they could sell for a huge profit. The Oba became worried about losing control of Benin and stopped contact with most European countries.

One of Benin's most valuable resources was rubber, which was made from the sap of the rubber tree. Rubber was in high demand in Europe at the end of the 19th century, as it was needed for bicycle tyres and shoes.

This illustration of the 'Benin Massacre', in which British troops were killed by soldiers from Benin, was published in a French newspaper in 1897.

Treaties and troops

In 1892, a British official travelled to Benin with a treaty that demanded control of all people and resources in Benin in exchange for the protection of the British Empire. It is very unlikely that the Oba signed this treaty, but the official claimed that he had. Five years later, a small group of British soldiers went to Benin to start taking control. Benin's army was waiting for them, and several British soldiers were killed. British soldiers called this the 'Benin Massacre'.

The British invasion

After the Benin Massacre, Britain sent more than 1,500 soldiers to invade Benin. They destroyed Benin City and stole many bronze plaques from the Oba's palace, which they claimed they needed to take in order to pay for the cost of the invasion of Benin. The Oba was sent into exile and Benin became part of the British Empire. Eventually, it became part of Nigeria, which gained independence in 1960.

Later, the descendants of the exiled Oba were allowed to return to Nigeria. This photo shows Oba Akenzua II, the grandfather of the current Oba, who ruled from 1933 to 1978.

Facts and figures

According to estimates, the walls around Benin City and the surrounding area measured 16,000 km in total and took around 150 million hours to build.

Although many pieces of art from Benin are called bronzes, they are not actually made from bronze. They are mainly made of brass, which is a mixture of copper and zinc.

When the slave trade was at its height, Benin sold 3,000 slaves a year. They continued to sell slaves until the late 19th century, by which point slavery had been banned in many countries.

The lungfish (a fish that can live on land and underwater) was an important animal in the culture of Benin. They were often shown on plaques alongside the Oba, as a sign of the Oba's power over land and sea.

Today there is a country called Benin, which has no connection to the Benin Kingdom. It is found to the west of Nigeria. The country is named after the Bight of Benin, a curve in the West African coastline, which got its name from the Benin Kingdom.

Around 3.8 million Edo people still live in the Benin Kingdom area of Nigeria.

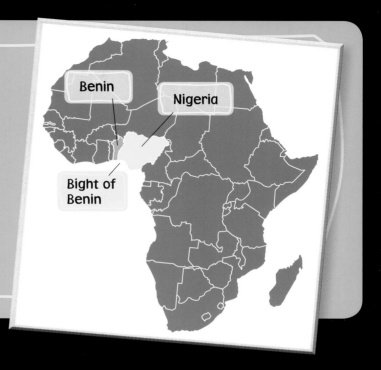

Timeline

After 900 CE	Groups of the Edo start living together and form the Igodomigodo kingdom.
12th century	The Ogisos lose control of Benin and the first Oba starts to rule.
1440	Benin begins to grow into a large, wealthy kingdom.
1485	The first Portuguese traders arrive in Benin.
19th century	European countries start to claim land in Africa.
1897	Britain invades Benin after the Benin Massacre and destroys Benin City.

Glossary

ancestors People from your family who lived a long time ago

artefact An object from the past that reveals information about the people who made it

CE The letters 'CE' stand for 'common era'. They refer to dates from CE 1.

coral A hard pink material made by a sea animal

ethnic group A group of people who belong to the same race

fictional Made-up or invented

guild An organisation of people who have the same job

imported Brought from another country

inhabitant Someone who lives in an area

ivory A hard material from the tusks of an elephant

merchant A person who travels around buying and selling goods

molten Melted

nobleman A powerful, rich man

official Someone who has an important job in the running of a country

plaque A flat piece of metal or stone that has writing or images on it

portrait A piece of art that is an image of someone

profit Money that you get from selling goods for more than you bought them for

resource Something that naturally occurs in a country and can be used, such as wood or stone

ritual A religious ceremony where certain actions are carried out

sacrifice To kill an animal because you believe it will make a god happy

sap A liquid found in the trunk of a tree

send into exile To force someone to live in another country

slave trade The buying and selling of slaves

symbolic Representing something

territory An area of land that is ruled by a particular leader or group of people

treaty A written agreement between two or more countries

Further reading

Benin Empire (Great Civilisations)
Catherine Chambers (Franklin Watts, 2016)

Benin 900–1897 CE (The History Detective Investigates),
Alice Harman (Wayland, 2015)

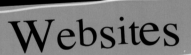

Websites

http://www.bbc.co.uk/ahistoryoftheworld/objects/rmAT6B7zTZCGACd7i7l6Wg
Listen to a BBC radio programme about a Benin bronze.

http://www.theschoolrun.com/homework-help/kingdom-benin
Find out 10 amazing facts about Benin.

http://www.britishmuseum.org/pdf/KingdomOfBenin_Presentation.pdf
Look at a presentation about Benin from the British Museum.

http://www.bbc.co.uk/guides/z3s2xnb
Learn more about life in the Benin Kingdom.

Index